DONALD J. SOBOL

Encyclopedia Brown
and the Case of
the Mysterious Handprints

Illustrated by Gail Owens

A BANTAM SKYLARK BOOK®
TORONTO • NEW YORK • LONDON • SYDNEY • AUCKLAND

For Josie and David Kenin

RL 3, 008–011

ENCYCLOPEDIA BROWN AND THE CASE OF THE MYSTERIOUS HANDPRINTS
A Bantam Skylark Book / February 1986

PRINTING HISTORY
William Morrow edition published September 1985

*Skylark Books is a registered trademark of Bantam Books,
Inc. Registered in U.S. Patent and Trademark Offices
and elsewhere.*

ISBN 0-553-15352-8

Published simultaneously in the United States and Canada

---

*Bantam Books are published by Bantam Books, Inc. Its trademark, consisting of the
words "Bantam Books" and the portrayal of a rooster, is Registered in U.S. Patent
and Trademark Office and in other countries. Marca Registrada. Bantam Books,
Inc., 666 Fifth Avenue, New York, New York 10103.*

PRINTED IN THE UNITED STATES OF AMERICA

CW   0 9 8 7 6 5 4 3 2 1

Contents

The Case of the Blond Wig

There was more to Idaville than met the eye.

To passing motorists, Idaville looked like an ordinary seaside town. It had lovely beaches, a Little League, and two delicatessens. It had churches, a synagogue, and four banks.

To police chiefs all over the country, however, Idaville was far from ordinary. No one got away with breaking a law in Idaville.

How did Idaville do it? What was the secret behind the town's spotless police record?

Only two grown-ups, Mr. and Mrs. Brown, knew the answer. Idaville's war on crime was masterminded by their only child, ten-year-old

Encyclopedia, America's Sherlock Holmes in sneakers.

Mr. Brown was the Idaville police chief. He was a fine officer, brave and smart. But sometimes he came up against a crime that even he could not solve. When that happened, he knew what to do. He drove home. At the dinner table he went over the facts of the case while Encyclopedia listened carefully.

Nothing else was necessary. Encyclopedia usually figured out the guilty person before dessert. If he needed a few minutes extra, his mother was disappointed.

Chief Brown hated keeping his son's sleuthing under cover. He would have liked the president to declare Encyclopedia a national treasure.

But if he told the truth, who would believe him?

Who would believe that the mastermind behind Idaville's crackdown on crime didn't look in the mirror after washing to see if his face was clean. He looked in his towel.

As for Encyclopedia, he never told anyone about the help he gave his father. He didn't want to seem different from other fifth-graders.

He was stuck with his nickname, however. Only his parents and teachers called him by

his real name, Leroy. Everyone else called him Encyclopedia.

An encyclopedia is a book or set of books filled with facts from A to Z. So was Encyclopedia's head. He had read more books than anyone in Idaville, and he never forgot what he read. His pals insisted that he was better than a library. They learned all kinds of things about books from him—such as footnotes don't come from squeaky shoes.

At the dinner table Friday evening, Chief Brown poked at his meat loaf. Encyclopedia and his mother knew what that meant. A case had him puzzled.

Chief Brown put down his fork. "There was trouble at the Yacht Club this morning," he said at last. "Someone smashed the rudder of *Defiance.*"

"Isn't *Defiance* one of the sailboats in the Commodore's Cup finals?" Mrs. Brown inquired.

"*Defiance* is racing *Childhood II,*" replied Chief Brown. "Whichever boat wins two out of three races will be awarded the Commodore's Cup for the year. Yesterday *Defiance* won the opening race."

Encyclopedia had read about the Commodore's Cup finals in the *Idaville News*. *Defiance* was owned and sailed by Mr. and Mrs. Ernest Day. *Childhood II* was owned and sailed by John Cushing and his brother, Tom. *Childhood II* was faster in light seas. *Defiance* was faster in rough seas. With Mr. Day at the helm, *Defiance* had sliced through angry waves yesterday to win by more than two minutes.

"Why don't you give Leroy the facts about the smashed rudder, dear," Mrs. Brown suggested. "He'll figure out who did it."

Chief Brown smiled and withdrew a small notebook from his breast pocket. "Here's what I have," he said.

At seven o'clock that morning, the night watchman at the Yacht Club went off duty. As he was leaving, a cleaning woman arrived. A few minutes later the woman glanced out the window and saw a blond man carrying a hammer. He was walking out on pier 2 toward the slip where *Defiance* was tied up. A light rain was falling.

The cleaning woman didn't bother about the man. Not more than ten minutes passed when she happened to glance out the same window. The pier was deserted. The man was gone.

Chief Brown said, "So far as I can tell, no one else was on the pier until eight o'clock. Then five or six men and women arrived to take out their boats. That's when the smashed rudder on *Defiance* was discovered."

"Do you think the blond man is responsible?" Mrs. Brown asked.

"Perhaps," Chief Brown answered cautiously. He flipped a page in his notebook.

"The manager of the Yacht Club telephoned Mr. Day, owner of *Defiance*," Chief Brown continued. "After examining the rudder himself, Mr. Day called me. He said the rudder couldn't be repaired in time for today's race, which was to start at noon. So the second race had to be postponed until tomorrow."

"That's a tough break for the Cushing brothers," Encyclopedia said. "The seas were calm today. *Childhood II* might have beaten *Defiance* and squared the series at one victory apiece."

"True," Chief Brown said. "But one of the brothers might have smashed the rudder, hoping that it could not be repaired at all."

"What a horrible example of sportsmanship," Mrs. Brown said. "I feel so sorry for the

Days. They're among the best-liked couples at the Yacht Club."

"I questioned the Cushing brothers," Chief Brown said. "They don't have an alibi for seven o'clock, when the blond man was on the pier. They insisted they were eating breakfast. They could be lying. They live alone, and no one saw them at breakfast."

"What about Mr. and Mrs. Day?" asked Mrs. Brown.

"Mr. Day said he and Mrs. Day were still sleeping at seven o'clock," answered Chief Brown. "Like the Cushing brothers, the Days live alone. And like the brothers, there is no one to support their story."

Chief Brown leafed through several pages of his notebook.

"Shortly before nine o'clock this morning," he said, "Mr. Day drove his wife to the beauty parlor. There is a supper dance at the Yacht Club tonight, and she wanted her hair set. Mr. Day said that he had just returned home when the phone rang. It was the manager of the Yacht Club calling. According to Mr. Day, that was when he learned about *Defiance*'s smashed rudder."

Mrs. Brown looked at Encyclopedia out of the corner of her eye. He had not asked his question. Usually he solved the toughest mystery with one question.

"If only the cleaning woman had recognized the man!" she declared.

"She saw only his back," Chief Brown said. "Oh, I nearly forgot. I found a blond wig on top of a trash can outside the kitchen of the Yacht Club. The cleaning woman swears the wig wasn't there when she came to work."

Mrs. Brown looked at Encyclopedia again. She seemed to expect him to solve the case now that he knew about the blond wig.

Encyclopedia had closed his eyes. He always closed his eyes when he did his deepest thinking on a case. But he wasn't ready yet to ask his one question.

So Mrs. Brown said, "What color hair do John and Tom Cushing have—and Mr. and Mrs. Day?"

"The Cushing brothers have dark hair," Chief Brown replied. "Mr. Day's hair is blond. Mrs. Day is a redhead."

Suddenly Encyclopedia opened his eyes. He asked his question. "Dad, did you check with the beauty parlor to see if Mr. Day drove his wife there this morning as he claims?"

"He told the truth," Chief Brown stated. "One of the beauticians saw him drive Mrs. Day up to the door."

"Leroy," Mrs. Brown exclaimed. "The rudder of the Days' sailboat was smashed around seven o'clock. They reached the beauty parlor some two hours later. What has one got to do with the other?"

"Everything, Mom," replied Encyclopedia.

WHY?

(*Turn to page 72 for the solution to
The Case of the Blond Wig.*)

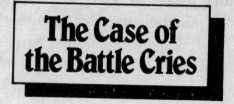

The Case of the Battle Cries

Encyclopedia did more than help his father solve mysteries. He helped the children of the neighborhood as well.

When school let out for the summer, he opened his own detective agency in the family garage. Every morning he hung out his sign:

BROWN
DETECTIVE AGENCY
13 Rover Avenue

LEROY BROWN
President

No case too small
25¢ per day plus expenses

The first customer Monday morning was Gary Hale. Encyclopedia was surprised to see him. Gary usually spent mornings at his hobby, entering contests.

So far this year, Gary had finished ninth in a national spark plug contest. He had won a free car wash in Pottstown, Pennsylvania. In several other contests he had won smaller prizes.

He laid twenty-five cents on the gas can beside Encyclopedia.

"I want to hire you," he said. "Bugs Meany just stole the words right out of my pocket."

"Trust Bugs to do something like that," Encyclopedia murmured.

Bugs Meany was the leader of a gang of tough older boys. They called themselves the Tigers. They should have called themselves the Pocket Watches. They always watched for the police while their hands went around in some little kid's pocket.

"Get back my words before Bugs wins a motorcycle," Gary said.

He explained. He had entered a contest, "Fighting Words of Famous Americans." Ten minutes ago he was hurrying to mail off his entry. Bugs Meany stopped him.

"Bugs asked me where I was going," Gary

said. "I made the mistake of telling him. Then I made a worse mistake. I told him first prize in the contest was a red, white, and blue motorcycle."

Gary had on a tan shirt with two buttonless pockets. Tapping his right pocket, he said, "I was carrying my contest entry here in an envelope. It stuck out. Bugs snatched it and walked off, chanting, 'Don't give up the ship!'"

"You're afraid Bugs will send in the sayings as his own?" Encyclopedia asked. "You're right. We'd better go and see him while there is still time."

"You go," Gary urged. "I didn't pay twenty-five cents to get a black eye."

"Steady up," Encyclopedia said. "I've handled Bugs before."

Gary hesitated, drew a deep breath, and shrugged. "Well . . . okay," he agreed. "I've always wanted to live dangerously."

The Tigers' clubhouse was an unused toolshed behind Mr. Sweeney's Auto Body Shop. Bugs was inside, alone.

"Make like Christopher Columbus," he growled at Encyclopedia, "and shove off."

"Gary claims you stole some famous sayings from him," the detective stated calmly.

"What?" Bugs cried. "Why, this kid is a world-class fruitcake. *He* stole the sayings from *me.*"

"How did he steal them, Bugs?" Encyclopedia inquired.

"Right from my shirt pocket," Bugs asserted.

"Your shirt doesn't have a pocket," Gary pointed out.

Bugs grunted as if he'd been clubbed over the head with a canoe. It took him a moment to find an answer.

"Cleanliness is dear to us Tigers," he said with a smirk. "In the summer we change our shirts twice a day. I was wearing a polo shirt with a pocket."

He traced a pocket over his right breast with his forefinger.

"My sayings were in an envelope, ready to be mailed," he continued. "The envelope stuck out of my pocket. This kid grabbed the envelope and ran."

"You thieving, lying crook!" Gary howled. "You should be elected president so you can grant yourself a pardon."

"Baby brain," growled Bugs, "don't make

me mad. Run along while I'm in my present good mood."

"I'm not budging till you return my sayings," Gary retorted. "In the words of William Travis, commander at the Alamo, 'I shall never surrender or retreat.' "

"Is that so?" Bugs jeered. "In the words of John Paul Jones, the naval hero, 'I have not yet begun to fight!' "

"Oh, yeah?" Gary shouted, " 'I propose to fight it out on this line if it takes all summer'—General U. S. Grant at the Battle of the Wilderness."

"Don't shout," Bugs cautioned. " 'Speak softly and carry a big stick'—President Theodore Roosevelt."

" 'Nuts!' " Gary roared. "General Anthony McAuliffe at the Battle of the Bulge!"

Bugs's face showed the strain of his struggle to keep up with Gary. The best he could squeeze out was "Remember the Pain!"

" 'Remember the *Maine*,' you big dummy," Gary corrected. " 'Remember the *Maine*' was the American battle cry against Spain."

"Uh-uh, I mean *pain*," Bugs said threateningly.

Gary stood firm. "You wouldn't know a single famous saying if you hadn't stolen them from me," he said, and spat his disgust.

Bugs raised a fist. "It isn't polite to spit, even if it's your own blood."

"Cool your jets, Bugs," Encyclopedia said. "I know you're the thief."

WHAT WAS BUGS'S MISTAKE?

*(Turn to page 74 for the solution to
The Case of the Battle Cries.)*

The Case of the Stolen Tools

The heart of Bugs Meany beat with a great desire. It was to get back at Encyclopedia.

Bugs hated being outsmarted all the time. He longed to lower Encyclopedia's IQ by yanking on his tonsils.

But Bugs never dared to use his size and strength. Whenever he felt the urge, he remembered Sally Kimball.

Sally was the prettiest girl in the fifth grade and the best athlete. She could do what no kid had thought was possible: punch out the Tigers' leader!

When they had fought last, Bugs went down

so often the ground ached. Between the bops
and the plops, he soon was too dizzy to know
where he was. He lay on his back and moaned,
"Let's form a committee."

After Sally joined the Brown Detective
Agency as a junior partner, Bugs quit trying to
bully Encyclopedia. Instead, he included Sally
in his plans for revenge.

"Bugs will try to get even for the lickings
you gave him," Encyclopedia warned her.

"Don't worry," Sally replied. "Bugs has a
big handicap, his brain. It's too odd to get
even."

The detectives were approaching Bugs's
house on their way to Joe Tully's birthday
party a block beyond. They began talking
about the party and the lively evening in store
for them.

The street was deserted. Above, a few stars
glimmered in the late twilight sky. The moon
was full.

The birthday party was fun piled upon fun.
After two hours, Sally received an unexpected
telephone call.

"That was Stan Hemming," she told Encyclopedia. "He asked us to come right over to
his house and use the back door. He doesn't

want to bother his folks. Bugs Meany stole his football."

Encyclopedia sighed. "I hate to leave the party. Still, if Stan needs help, we'd better go."

Stan lived next door to Bugs. A row of thick, high bushes separated the two properties. No lights shone from Stan's house as the detectives entered the backyard.

Encyclopedia caught Sally's arm. "Are you sure it was really Stan who telephoned —"

"There they are, the dirty little thieves!"

Bugs Meany strode from behind a storage shed. Officer Clancy was with him.

"They've come back for the loot!" Bugs cried.

"Bugs claims you broke into the Hemmings' storage shed a couple of hours ago," Officer Clancy declared.

Sally glared at Bugs. "You liar! I'd wring your neck if you'd wash it."

"Save the fast lip for the judge," Bugs jeered. "Your secret life of crime is over!"

"Simmer down, both of you," Officer Clancy ordered. "Tell them what you told me, Bugs. The truth, now."

"I heard them talking about the Hemmings being away on vacation as they passed my house two hours ago," Bugs began. "They decided this was their big chance. They slipped into the backyard, broke into the storage shed, and removed some power tools."

Bugs paused for effect. He drew himself up as straight as George Washington taking the oath of office.

"Miss Muscles wanted to scram with the loot," he went on. "Mr. Know-It-All said they'd better show up at Joe Tully's party. They could leave early and come back for the tools. And here they are!"

Office Clancy pointed to a stack of firewood beside the storage shed. "Bugs and I found an edger, a trimmer, and a leaf-blower hidden there," he said.

"How could you see the storage shed, Bugs?" Encyclopedia demanded. "The bushes are in the way."

Bugs grinned as if he'd been waiting for the question. "I saw *over* the bushes. Have a look yourself."

He led Officer Clancy and the detectives into his house, up the stairs, and onto the second-floor porch.

From the porch Encyclopedia had a clear, moonlit view of Stan Hemming's backyard.

"Before my folks went out tonight," Bugs said, "Dad lent me his telescope. I was studying the moon when these missing links walked by, plotting."

In the middle of the porch stood a small telescope. It was pointed at the sky.

"My hobby is studying the heavens," Bugs announced in a voice dripping with sincerity. "I have such a hunger for knowledge."

"Sit down before you faint of starvation," Sally snapped. "You placed the telescope here just to make your story ring true. You couldn't tell a full moon from a corn muffin."

While Bugs groped for a retort, Sally peered through the telescope—and stepped back in surprise.

"He *was* looking at the moon. I saw it clearly," she told Encyclopedia.

Bugs crowed, "While they were stealing the tools, I raced downstairs and called the police. Then I hid behind the bushes and waited for them to return from the party. If you hadn't arrived, Officer Clancy, I'd have made a citizen's arrest. Us Tigers know our duty."

"You telephoned me to come here," Sally said. "You pretended to be Stan Hemming. You're trying to frame us!"

"Listen to her rave," Bugs said. "Brain surgery isn't for everyone, but this dame is ready."

Officer Clancy held up his hand. "We'll settle this at headquarters."

"That won't be necessary," Encyclopedia said. "I can prove Bugs is lying."

WHAT WAS THE PROOF?

(Turn to page 76 for the solution to The Case of the Stolen Tools.)

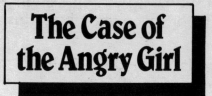

The Case of the Angry Girl

Tyrone Taylor had a way with the gentle sex.

He was forever typing notes and poems to girls of his choice.

When Encyclopedia and Sally saw him in South Park on Saturday afternoon, he wasn't typing. He was tipping. He was standing before a bench, bowing and tipping his hat.

"He's practicing to be Mr. Polite," Sally whispered. "I'll bet he's meeting a girl."

Tyrone spied the detectives and motioned them over.

"Which greeting do you like better?" he inquired of Sally. "This?" He lifted his hat a few inches off his head. "Or this?" He swept his hat off grandly and bowed to the knees.

"I like the first one," Sally answered. "The other makes you look as though you're shoveling flies."

"Good," Tyrone approved. "I like the simple approach better myself. It's more refined."

Suddenly he stooped to pick a sunflower. "The perfect touch!" he exclaimed. He sat down on the bench, holding the sunflower like a vase of roses.

"What's this all about, Tyrone?" Encyclopedia asked.

"I'm meeting Adorabelle Walsh here any minute," Tyrone answered. "I have to treat her like a lady."

Encyclopedia understood. It wasn't wise to forget your manners around Adorabelle.

Adorabelle was a fifth-grader with a special talent, a strong right arm. At the last Junior Olympics, she had won the girls' shotput.

"Here she comes now," Sally remarked.

"We'll leave you alone," Encyclopedia told Tyrone. "We're overdue at the field for a softball game."

"Good luck," Tyrone said. "I hope you win."

"I hope you win, too," Sally replied with a smile.

The detectives had walked fifty yards when Sally tugged Encyclopedia behind a bush. "Let's hide. I just *have* to see Tyrone in action," she confessed.

In the next eight seconds, there was plenty of action—most of it by Adorabelle.

Tyrone jumped to his feet, tipped his hat, and offered the sunflower.

Adorabelle ignored it. She stepped in close and landed a right on Tyrone's jaw, spinning his hat halfway around his head. Then, *thud*! She buried her left in his stomach.

Tyrone sank to the earth, nose down. It was all over before the detectives knew what was happening.

Sally gasped, "That is one angry girl!"

"And very neat, too," Encyclopedia added as he watched Adorabelle clean up.

Adorabelle dragged Tyrone onto the bench and laid him out, toes up. She folded his arms over his chest, tucked his hat under his hands, and placed the sunflower between his teeth.

"Go find a cushion, you pinhead!" she flung at the speechless figure, and marched off.

When Sally and Encyclopedia reached him, Tyrone was just coming around. He gagged.

Sally removed the sunflower from his mouth. "You poor boy," she murmured. "How do you feel?"

Tyrone groaned. "If I felt any better, I'd get to a hospital."

"Whatever made Adorabelle so angry?" Sally asked.

Tyrone groaned again. "All I did was write her this note." He fumbled a sheet from his pocket and gave it to Encyclopedia.

The detective read the typewritten words.

How I long for a girl who understands what true romance is all about. You are sweet and faithful. Girls who are unlike you kiss the first boy who comes along, Adorabelle. I'd like to praise your beauty forever. I can't stop thinking you are the prettiest girl alive. Thine,

Tyrone

"You've written better," Encyclopedia said. "It's choppy, but it isn't *that* bad."

"I borrowed some sentences from a book of love letters and strung them together," Tyrone admitted. "I was kind of in a rush."

He explained. Adorabelle was leaving that night for a week in Atlanta. He had dashed off the letter three hours ago to express his feelings for her.

"I called her at noon," Tyrone said. "I expected to read the letter over the telephone as if the words had just come to me. She wasn't home. So I spoke with Lulubelle, her kid sister. Lulubelle took down what I said and promised to give the message to Adorabelle."

"Lulubelle is only in third grade," Sally protested. "She must have got the words wrong. Or maybe she changed them because she doesn't like you."

"She likes me," Tyrone insisted. "She's taken messages before, and she prints clearly in capital letters. Besides, I had her repeat each word as she took it down."

He fingered his bruised jaw a moment before continuing.

"Adorabelle called me an hour ago," he said. "She had received my message. She asked to meet me here. Oh, my, did she sound eager."

"She was eager to pop your bulb," Sally said. "Encyclopedia, what went wrong for Tyrone?"

The detective didn't answer. He was reading the letter again. Understanding flickered across his face.

"Kid sister Lulubelle meant well," he murmured. "But I'm afraid she is to blame."

WHY?

*(Turn to page 78 for the solution to
The Case of the Angry Girl.)*

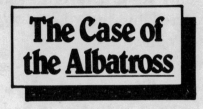

The Case of the Albatross

Encyclopedia and Sally entered the Idaville Trout Fishing Tournament for Children because of Conway Tintushel.

Conway had a boat.

Encyclopedia fished with Conway several times a summer and always paid a painful price. Along with a few snapper and grouper, the detective caught an earache. Conway, a kind but gabby sixth-grader, talked a better line than he fished.

The trout tournament began Thursday morning as the sun cleared the horizon. The starter's whistle sent twenty-three boats racing across the bay toward favorite fishing spots. Conway steered his little boat, *Albatross*, for Lighthouse Point.

"Last week I discovered the grass beds there," he said. "You should have seen a trout I landed. I took a picture of it, and the negative weighed eight pounds. Lighthouse Point is my secret spot."

A few others knew the secret. Half a dozen boats were strung out over the grass beds when *Albatross* chugged up.

Conway killed the motor and let *Albatross* drift.

"Fish," he announced, "if you're looking for a fight, here I am."

After half an hour, he had caught a snapper and Sally had caught a grouper. Neither was big enough to keep.

"Fishing can be a spectator sport," Encyclopedia mused as he waited for his first nibble.

"The tide is wrong," Conway complained. "Let's try another spot I know—Biscayne Landing. We'll haul in so many trout, our elbows will hurt."

Biscayne Landing was deserted, except for fish. They began biting almost immediately.

"Lock the doors. They're coming in the

windows!" Conway cried gleefully as he reeled in a trout. "This is the hot spot!"

Within ten minutes three small trout, three groupers, and a snapper lay in the ice chest.

Encyclopedia had hooked into his second trout when everything changed. A twenty-four-foot sportfisherman raced directly at *Albatross*.

"That's Jim Loring's boat," Sally said. *"What's he doing?"*

At the last second the sportfisherman swerved, narrowly missing *Albatross,* and glided to a halt.

Sally gazed in disbelief at Jim and the two teenage boys with him. "Those cement-heads. They nearly hit us!"

"Ignore them," Encyclopedia advised. "Let's fish."

"Not here," Conway declared angrily. "Jim just scared all the fish away."

Conway hoisted anchor, and for the next three hours he looked in at one fishing spot after another. At eleven o'clock he headed for the docks. The tournament ended at noon.

Albatross was among the last boats to return. After tying up, the three children reported to the judges' table.

Benny Breslin, one of Encyclopedia's pals, was helping weigh the trout. "Any luck?" he inquired.

"Pompeii was luckier," Sally said. "We caught five small trout. And some grouper and snapper by mistake."

"Who's in the lead?" Conway asked.

"Jim Loring looks like the sure winner," Benny answered sadly.

"Impossible," Encyclopedia said. "The tournament is for kids fifteen and under. Today is Jim's sixteenth birthday."

"Not all day," Benny corrected. "Jim convinced the judges that he was born in the evening. So he won't be sixteen for a few hours yet."

"The big hunk of baloney!" Conway screamed. "Only his eyebrows keep him from being a barefaced liar!"

"Jim told me that he caught his biggest trout off Biscayne Landing," Benny said. "He claimed you three saw him do it."

Benny searched among the papers on the table in front of him. He found a color photograph and handed it to Encyclopedia.

"This is a picture of Jim catching the trout," Benny said. "It was taken with his new high-speed camera that develops its own color prints."

Encyclopedia, Sally, and Conway stared at the photograph. It showed a bowed fishing rod off the stern of a boat. In the air a foot above the water was a trout. Its tail was turned up in the familiar curve of a hooked fish struggling against a line. The details were so sharp that Encyclopedia could see the line and even the drops of water as they dripped downward from the fish.

"You can't tell who is catching the fish," Sally objected. "Jim isn't in the picture."

"No, he isn't," Benny said. "But take a closer look. Notice the boat in the background."

There was another boat in the picture. Although it was in the distance and somewhat out of focus, the boat did look like *Albatross*. And the three blurred figures in the boat wore the same color clothing as Encyclopedia, Sally, and Conway.

"Jim left the picture with the judges to prove you were present when he caught it," Benny said. "You're his witnesses."

"Encyclopedia," Sally said anxiously, "you've got to prove the picture is a fake!"

Encyclopedia studied the photograph more closely.

"The fish is the only hard part," he said. "The rest of the case is easy."

WHAT DID HE MEAN?

(*Turn to page 80 for the solution to
The Case of the* <u>Albatross</u>.)

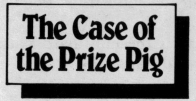

The Case of the Prize Pig

Encyclopedia and Sally were worried. Their bus was an hour late reaching the fairgrounds.

"Golly, I hope we haven't missed seeing Hambone run," Sally said.

Hambone, a young racing pig, was trained by Lucy Fibbs, a classmate of the detectives. Lucy lived on a farm. She loved all animals, but pigs were her favorites. "Pigs don't get any respect," she often complained.

"Hambone will get plenty of respect if he wins today," Encyclopedia told Sally.

The huge tents of the Farm Progress Show

stood in a circle on the fairgrounds. Hurrying through the parking lot, the detectives came upon Chuck Dawson. He was tying his shoe-lace beside his motorcycle.

"Are the pigs still racing?" Sally asked him.

"Don't know," Chuck answered. "I just got here myself."

Chuck was nineteen, the son of a tobacco farmer. His motorcycle was painted tobacco-leaf brown, and he was never without a cigar.

"I'm glad you're here," he said. "My dad's fastest pig, Upset Tummy, is entered in the races. I've a hunch there may be dirty work."

"What makes you think that?" inquired Encyclopedia.

"Whichever pig wins will be worth a barrel of money," Chuck replied. He flicked the long ash off his cigar, lighted it, and puffed. "What say we join forces and keep watch for any funny business."

Encyclopedia agreed. If trouble came, he wanted Chuck on his side, with or without a cigar.

At the pig-racing tent, Chuck stationed himself by the entrance. The detectives went inside and looked for Lucy Fibbs and Ham-bone.

Most of the tent was occupied by a half-oval track surrounded by wood stands. Pig fans filled every seat.

Not a pig was in sight. Encyclopedia and Sally worked their way to the staging area in the rear. They found Lucy and Hambone in the third stall on the right.

"How'd you like my Hambone's speed?" Lucy asked, beaming.

"We just arrived," Sally replied sheepishly.

"Not to worry," Lucy said. "You'll see Hambone run in the final. He won his heat in three and a half seconds flat, a track record."

She finished pinning a big number "1" onto Hambone's racing silks of maroon and gray.

"In the final, Hambone will start in chute number one because he had the fastest time in the heats," she said.

She gave Hambone a loving pat and hug. Then she launched into her favorite subject, pig racing.

"A farmer begins with ten or twelve three-month-old piglets," she explained. "For six hours a day the little porkers are trained to start at the sound of a bell. They race to a trough with a chocolate chip cookie in it."

"That must wear you out," Sally said.

"No, pigs are easy to train," Lucy replied. "They are humble, even-tempered, and smarter than dogs."

A man in a dark suit shouted, "Two minutes to post time."

Lucy gave the leash around Hambone's neck a gentle tug. "Stay close to me," she whispered to the detectives. "I'll say you're my assistant trainers."

Encyclopedia and Sally joined Lucy and Hambone in the pig parade to the track. At the starting line were four chutes, large plywood boxes with an overhead door at each end. An air slot six inches long and an inch wide was cut into the top of each chute.

Encyclopedia had a minute to study the other three racers and their trainers.

At chute number two was Fast Fatso, trained by Mrs. Markin. Fast Fatso seemed excited. Mrs. Markin seemed nervous. She kept glancing over at Hambone.

At chute number three was Greasy Lightning, trained by Mr. Heston, who was chewing yellow bubble gum.

At chute number four was Upset Tummy, trained by Mr. Dawson, Chuck Dawson's father. Mr. Dawson was speaking into Upset Tummy's right ear.

"Runners, take your mark," the starter hollered.

Lucy removed the leash from Hambone's neck. Immediately Hambone darted through the open rear door and into the chute.

"Strange, he usually doesn't like to get *into* the chute," Lucy remarked. She let the rear door drop closed.

Within seconds all the pigs had disappeared into the chutes. The starter rang a bell. At the same time he pulled a rope that opened the front doors of the four chutes.

The huge tent shook with cries of *"They're off!"*

Hambone never had a chance. He broke from his chute late and couldn't make up ground. Mrs. Markin's Fast Fatso took the win in 4.12 seconds and the chocolate chip cookie at the finish line even faster. Hambone wound up last.

Lucy was stunned. "Hambone always makes such a great start," she murmured. "I don't understand. . . ."

While Sally tried to comfort her, Encyclopedia examined the top of Hambone's chute. He had noticed a speck of brown on the edge of the air slot. He sniffed . . . chocolate!

"Did you find something?" Sally asked anxiously.

"I found the reason for Hambone's bad start," Encyclopedia said, "and the person responsible. To think I nearly missed one of the clues!"

WHAT DID ENCYCLOPEDIA MEAN?

(*Turn to page 82 for the solution to
The Case of the Prize Pig.*)

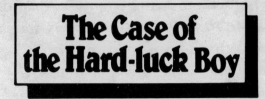

The Case of the Hard-luck Boy

Arty Yakamoto came into the Brown Detective Agency. He was smiling.

Immediately Encyclopedia knew something was wrong.

Arty smiled only when he suffered. Hard luck followed him like the seat of his pants. If a day went well, he was disappointed.

"What's the bad news today, Arty?" Encyclopedia asked.

"For starters, it's my birthday," Arty replied. "I'm eleven today."

"Happy birthday," Sally said.

Arty winced. "Happy? No chance. I'm already halfway to being twenty-two, and that's halfway to forty-four. Yuck! Forty-four is *middle-aged*. What's happened to my life?"

"Arty, you don't need a detective," Sally declared. "You need a longer calendar."

"I'm not here because of my age," Arty said. "I'm here because of my vocabulary."

He explained. The Friends of the Library had a birthday that day, too. The club was six years old. As part of the celebration, the women were holding a vocabulary quiz. Any sixth-grader who held a job could enter. Arty worked at his family's furniture store.

"I'll win," Arty said, "if I can beat Mary McKean, Peggy Olsen, and Herb Levy. They're the word brains."

Encyclopedia knew the three. Mary McKean called herself a bookkeeper because she straightened the shelves in her father's bookstore after school. Peggy Olsen helped her teenage brother with his summer lawn business. Herb Levy had a year-round newspaper route.

Arty counted out twenty-five cents.

"The vocabulary quiz starts in twenty minutes," he said. "I want to hire you to look after

my interests. With my luck, I could lose even if
I win."

"We'll take the case," Encyclopedia said,
and wondered what Arty was talking about.
The "case" had neither a crime nor a mystery.

The Friends of the Library rented rooms in
a house on Worth Street. The detectives and
Arty arrived with five minutes to spare.

Encyclopedia spent a minute taking note of
the ground-floor layout. Four rooms and a
bathroom opened off the center hall. At the far
end, a water cooler stood beside a staircase.

Most of the contestants were crowded before
one of the rooms. They chattered about what
the prizes might be. Encyclopedia rose on tip-
toes and peeked in.

He saw three boxes on a desk. A card
marked each box clearly: FIRST PRIZE, SECOND
PRIZE, THIRD PRIZE.

Mrs. Fuller, the club president, came down
the stairs. "Time to begin, children," she
called, waving the quiz sheets. "Everyone else
outside, please."

She herded the contestants into the largest
room. Encyclopedia and Sally moved outside.

During the fifty minutes that the quiz
lasted, Encyclopedia watched the front door of

the house. Sally watched the back. No one went in or out of the building.

When Arty appeared, it was obvious that he had done well. He looked disappointed.

"No sense in your hanging around," he said to the detectives. "The winners won't be announced for an hour at least. I'll let you know if I win anything."

Encyclopedia and Sally returned to the detective agency. They felt funny. They had done nothing to earn their fee.

They felt worse when Arty came by later that afternoon. He was smiling.

"I told you it would happen," he said in a voice heavy enough to sink a ship in dry dock. "I won, but I lost."

He held out his first prize, a wristwatch. It was broken.

"It was broken when I opened the box," Arty said.

Encyclopedia and Sally stared in disbelief. Then they began questioning Arty. He told them what he knew.

The prizes had been handed out in reverse order. Herb Levy was awarded third prize, a bicycle light. Next, Mary McKean was awarded second prize, a small adding machine. Finally, Arty received the broken wrist-watch. True to his nature, he had accepted his fate and told no one.

Afterward, though, he had spoken with Mrs. Fuller, the club president. He learned that she had inspected the prizes that morning. They were in perfect condition. She had not, however, checked them again before the awards ceremony.

Mrs. Fuller had supervised the quiz. She had allowed one child at a time to leave the room for a few minutes. Unfortunately, Arty hadn't noticed which kids left the room. He'd been busy answering questions.

"There were ten questions," he said. "Herb Levy missed the second question and half of the last question. Mary McKean missed all of the last question. I missed only half of the last question."

"The last question must have been tough," Sally observed. "What was it?"

"The first half was to write a word with two double letters in a row," Arty replied. "I put down, 'balloon,' and so did Herb Levy."

"And the second half?" asked Encyclopedia.

"You had to write a word with *three* double

letters in a row," Arty said. "Everyone flunked that half."

Sally looked at Encyclopedia. "We should give Arty back his twenty-five cents. We didn't help him."

"Wrong," corrected Encyclopedia. "We can help him. I know who broke the wristwatch."

WHO?

*(Turn to page 84 for the solution to
The Case of the Hard-luck Boy.)*

The Case of
the Giant Watermelon

Encyclopedia and Sally were tossing a bas-ketball Saturday morning when Omar Boxlittler telephoned.

"Encyclopedia, I need you!" Omar wailed. "Milly-Dilly has been stolen!"

All summer the kids in the neighborhood had been hearing reports about Milly-Dilly. She was a watermelon, the superstar of Omar's melon patch.

"I'll be right over," Encyclopedia promised. To Sally he said, "This could be a juicy case."

The detectives rode the number nine bus to the farmlands north of town. Omar met them at the stop near his home. He looked so down at the mouth that Encyclopedia could scarcely see his chin.

Omar mumbled a greeting and led the detectives across ripening fields to a patch of ground behind his house. The ground was covered with huge watermelons. The biggest lay under tents.

"Dad let me have the patch last year on my tenth birthday," Omar said. "The soil is too sandy for a cash crop. He wanted to see what I could grow."

"They're the largest watermelons I've ever seen," Sally said in amazement.

"The ordinary store watermelon weighs between eighteen and thirty pounds. The smallest one in my crop this year is a hundred and twenty pounds," Omar said proudly.

"What's your secret?" Encyclopedia asked.

"The seed," Omar answered. "The seed makes the difference, plus the right amount of water. For a good fertilizer, I use my mom's horse, Milly."

He stared at the watermelons a moment. "I owe a lot to Milly," he said solemnly.

"Do giant watermelons sell well?" Sally inquired.

"No way," replied Omar. "They're hard to ship, and buyers don't like lugging them from the supermarket. I raise them just for the shows."

"There must be a lot of money in the shows," Sally observed.

Omar shook his head. "The winners get only ribbons. But one seed from a champion can bring more than the price of a necktie. Of course, there's always some cash in spitting."

He explained. Last year's county champion, Mr. Keil, sold several seeds from his prize watermelon to spitters. They took them to the national watermelon spitting championship in Wisconsin.

"Using his seeds, Anna and Ada Bemus placed second in the two-person spit," Omar said. "They had a combined distance of fifty-two feet, one inch."

"No wonder someone snatched Milly-Dilly," Sally said. "Where was she growing?"

Omar pointed to an empty tent. "I keep the fastest growers under tents to avoid sunburn," he said. "Yesterday Milly-Dilly weighed in at a hundred and sixty-four pounds. She was growing at the rate of three pounds a day. Sometimes in the evening I'd sit here and drink a root beer and watch her grow. . . ."

His voice faltered. He suddenly seemed near to tears.

Recovering himself, he said, "I planned to enter her in the watermelon festival in Glenn City on Monday. Even if she didn't win, I'd keep her seeds. I reckoned that in three years I'd be able to produce a two-hundred-pounder."

"Whom do you suspect?" Encyclopedia asked.

"Russ Dallas, Clive Huey, or Dave Longsbury," Omar answered. "They're high school kids who live on farms near here. They grow watermelons for size, too."

"How about clues?" Sally asked.

"I found a book in the bushes down by the road," Omar said. "Wait a second."

He ran into the house and came back with the book. He handed it to Encyclopedia.

Encyclopedia read the title: *Fifty Greatest Baseball Players of the Twentieth Century.*

"Dave, Clive, and Russ have been checking on Milly-Dilly every day," Omar said. "The way I see it, one of them took to hiding in the bushes, waiting for my folks and me to leave the house together. He read the book to pass the time. Last evening we all went out to dinner. He sneaked behind the house, cut Milly-Dilly from the vine, and made off with her. Then—"

"He hid her in the bushes by the road," Sally broke in, "while he went for his truck. But he forgot about the book and left it behind. Doesn't that make sense, Encyclopedia?"

Encyclopedia rubbed his chin thoughtfully. "Which one of the three boys follows baseball?"

"They're all baseball nuts," Omar answered. "And they all have heroes. Babe Ruth is Dave's, Ty Cobb is Russ's, and Ted Williams is Clive's."

Encyclopedia opened the book and glanced down the table of contents. There were chapters on Babe Ruth, Ty Cobb, and Ted Williams.

"The thief was afraid Milly-Dilly would beat his watermelon at the festival on Monday," Sally grumbled. "Let's question Dave and Russ and Clive."

"Not without some proof," objected Omar, "or we'll wake up with our eyes shut before we go to bed. Don't forget, the thief carried Milly-Dilly down to the road. He's *strong*."

Sally kicked the ground and exclaimed,

"We just can't give up. Encyclopedia, think of something!"

"I already have," said the detective. "A simple test ought to show us who is guilty."

WHAT WAS THE TEST?

(*Turn to page 86 for the solution to The Case of the Giant Watermelon.*)

The Case of the Fighter Kite

On Friday the rain did not stop falling until three o'clock in the afternoon.

"Let's go to the beach," Sally suggested. "No one else will be there."

Sally was wrong. Merwin Elkberry was there.

Merwin, a sixth-grader, never had to be told to go fly a kite. At the slightest hint of a breeze, he was out scraping the sky with a kite or two.

When the detectives spied him, Merwin was kiting—and fishing. He was using a yellow kite to lift his surf-casting line behind the breakers.

"Any luck?" Encyclopedia asked.

"Two nibbles," Merwin answered, as happy as if he'd caught a school of kingfish.

"Gosh, Merwin," Sally said. "You've got your world on a string."

"There's nothing like kiting," Merwin replied. "I brought along my fighter just in case the fish went to the movies. Here, hold this and I'll show you."

He handed Sally his fishing pole. From a sack on the sand beside him, he withdrew a strange red kite.

"It's an Indian fighting kite," he said. "You can't really call kite flying the national sport of India, but everyone does it."

The red kite was unlike the usual American kites. It was smaller and lighter. Its string was glass-coated.

"A fighter can fly rings around an ordinary kite," Merwin asserted.

With three steps and an expert sweep of his arm, he sent the red fighter aloft in the strong wind.

"You win a fight," he said, "if you can work your kite below the other kite and cut its string. Then, if you can wrap its loose string around the string of your kite, the other kite is yours to keep."

"You may have a chance to demonstrate," Sally remarked. "Look over there."

From behind a point of land to the north a blue fighter kite had appeared. It climbed swiftly. Soon it vanished into the heavy, low clouds.

"Hey, that's dangerous!" Merwin gasped.

Encyclopedia knew what he meant. Small private planes regularly followed the coastline to the airport. A kite could jam an engine. . . .

"I'll bring down that nitwit," Merwin vowed. He let his red fighter sail higher. With two short tugs he signaled a challenge.

The blue fighter responded. It dived below the clouds as if to do battle.

Merwin was guiding his kite into position for combat when Sally hollered, "I've got one!" The fishing rod in her hands was bent and trembling.

For the next few minutes, the war in the sky was forgotten. The two boys showered Sally with advice.

It was all for nothing. The fishing rod snapped straight. Sally groaned. "I've lost him."

"So did I," Merwin said. His red fighter floated alone in the sky. The blue fighter had been reeled in.

"I'm going to find out who's to blame for flying a kite into the clouds," Merwin swore.

"We'll help you," Sally volunteered.

"Four people in Idaville fly blue fighters," Merwin said. "Three are grown-ups who kite only on weekends. That leaves Tessie Bottoms."

The detectives waited while Merwin parked his kites and fishing gear in the Beach Patrol office. Then all three biked to Tessie's house.

No one answered the doorbell. Merwin rang again.

"Stay alert, Encyclopedia," Sally warned. "Tessie is the worst liar in eighth grade. When she feeds her dogs, her mother has to call them."

"She could move in the best circles without going straight," put in Merwin. "At the kite club's tournament in May, she tripped two opponents. She was suspended for six months."

The door opened. Tessie peered out suspiciously. She wore a bathrobe and slippers. "What is it?"

Sally put it to her right away. "Didn't you fly a blue kite into the clouds this afternoon?"

Tessie's nose went up. "Whatever makes you think so?"

"Where were you for the past hour?" Sally persisted.

"Taking a bubble bath," Tessie said. "I was drying off when the door bell rang."

"The bubble bath didn't do any good," Merwin whispered to Encyclopedia. "Her face still looks as if it were left out all night."

"You soaked in the tub for an *hour?*" Sally exclaimed.

"Longer—I must be beautiful tonight," Tessie declared. "I have a heavy date."

"What a laugh," Merwin said under his breath. "Not even the tide would take her out."

Tessie withdrew a fingernail file from the pocket of her bathrobe. As if to show how weary she was of the conversation, she began to file the nails on her left hand.

"You little squirts must be hard up for action," she said in a bored voice. "Go find something better to do than make up stories about a blue kite in the clouds."

"Would you rather we report you to the airport officials?" Encyclopedia inquired. "Your alibi is all wet, Tessie!"

WHAT WAS TESSIE'S MISTAKE?

*(Turn to page 88 for the solution to
The Case of the Fighter Kite.)*

The Case of the Mysterious Handprints

On Sunday afternoon Encyclopedia received the treat of treats. He went with his father on a real police case.

Clarence Heiden had reported a pair of valuable bookends missing. He had asked Chief Brown to investigate the theft personally.

Every kid in town knew of Mr. Heiden. Fifty years ago he had started his career selling cotton candy in a circus. By the time he retired to Idaville, he owned circuses in the United States, Canada, and Mexico.

A bachelor, Mr. Heiden lived with three servants in a rambling old house. His grounds, which backed onto a canal, were surrounded by a wire fence.

He was waiting on the front porch when Chief Brown and Encyclopedia drove up.

"Thank you for coming out on a Sunday," he said to Chief Brown. "This must be your son, Leroy."

Encyclopedia liked him right away. Instead of pinching the young detective's cheek, he shook hands.

"The bookends mean a lot to me," Mr. Heiden said. "Since they're made of ivory, I expect they're worth a great deal. To me they're priceless. They were a gift from my office staff when I retired."

"When did you notice that they were missing?" inquired Chief Brown.

"About seven o'clock this morning," Mr. Heiden answered. "I keep them on my desk in the den. They must have been stolen during the night."

The heaviest thunderstorm of the summer had struck Idaville the night before. Encyclopedia had read about it in the *Idaville News.* The rains had begun around midnight and had not stopped until nearly dawn.

"Do you suspect anyone?" Chief Brown asked. "One of your servants, perhaps?"

"No, no," Mr. Heiden said emphatically. "They've been with me for years. If they wanted the bookends, they could have stolen them long ago."

"Who else might have slipped into the den last night?" Chief Brown asked.

"My two houseguests." Mr. Heiden spoke reluctantly. "The thief might be either of them, but I hope that I'm mistaken."

He explained. The guests, Molly Farrow and Jack Maloney, were old friends from his early circus days. Miss Farrow had been a bareback rider and later a seamstress with the circus. Mr. Maloney had been an acrobat until he lost the use of his feet in an automobile accident.

"Come inside and I'll introduce you," Mr. Heiden said.

Miss Farrow and Mr. Maloney were in the living room playing chess. Miss Farrow was a thin woman with small, quick hands. Mr. Maloney, a large man, sat in a wheelchair.

Neither seemed nervous under Chief Brown's questioning. Both insisted they had nothing to do with the theft of the bookends.

From the living room, Mr. Heiden led Chief Brown and Encyclopedia to the kitchen at the rear of the house. Through the kitchen window Encyclopedia saw a guest cottage. It had two doors that opened onto a front porch. The front porch faced the back porch of the main house.

"The cottage was finished last week," Mr. Heiden said. "It contains two units, each with a bedroom and a bath. Molly is staying in the unit on the right. Jack has the one on the left. As you can see, I haven't yet laid down sod."

Bare earth stretched between the cottage and the main house, a distance of fifty yards. The thunderstorm had churned the earth into mud.

Mr. Heiden opened the kitchen door and stepped onto the back porch.

"I sometimes forget to lock this door," he admitted. "I'm afraid it was left unlocked last night. I want to show you something quite strange."

He pointed to two trails of handprints in the mud. The handprints went between the back porch of the house and the front porch of the cottage, one set in each direction.

"It looks like someone walked on his hands,"

Chief Brown said. "Why? Was anything else stolen?"

"Yesterday morning," Mr. Heiden replied, "my handyman reported that a pair of work gloves and a small bag of ready-mix cement were missing. An hour later Molly said she couldn't find her leather dress gloves."

"Did you search the cottage?" Chief Brown asked.

"Molly and Jack demanded a search," Mr. Heiden said. "I found none of the missing articles in their rooms."

Beside the handprints, the only marks in the rain-washed earth between the cottage and house were wheel tracks and a set of woman's footprints.

"Those were made this morning," Mr. Heiden said. "Coming to breakfast, Molly had to help Jack with his wheelchair because of the mud."

Encyclopedia had heard enough. He believed he knew who had stolen the bookends, but he wanted to be sure.

He excused himself and strolled behind the cottage.

Six feet from the back doors ran a wire fence

that surrounded Mr. Heiden's grounds. A few feet beyond the fence flowed the canal.

"Throwing distance," Encyclopedia thought. "The thief has to be—"

WHO?

(Turn to page 90 for the solution to The Case of the Mysterious Handprints.)

Solution to
The Case of the Blond Wig

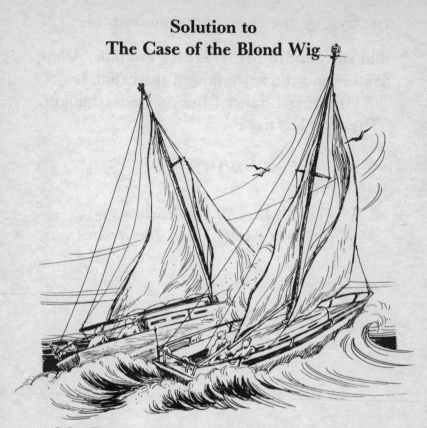

Mr. Day wanted the second race postponed. The calm sea favored the Cushings' boat.

However, he didn't want to commit a crime by damaging their boat. So he damaged his own. He wore a blond wig and left it where it would be found. Since he was a blond, he thought to cast suspicion on the dark-haired Cushings.

He claimed that he first learned about the smashed rudder when the Yacht Club manager telephoned him—*after* he had driven Mrs. Day to have her hair set. Therefore, as Encyclopedia realized, the Days *already* knew the race would be postponed.

Mrs. Day would never have had her hair set a few hours before competing in a sailboat race. Her new hairdo would have blown apart in the wind!

Solution to
The Case of the Battle Cries

Bugs remembered that he had stolen the sayings from Gary's right-hand shirt pocket. But he forgot Gary's shirt had *two* pockets.

When he accused Gary of stealing the sayings from him, he had to think fast. The shirt he had on did not have a pocket.

So he made up the story about having on a different shirt at the time of the theft—one with "a pocket." He traced the pocket on his right side. That was his mistake!

If a man's or boy's shirt has only one pocket, it is on the wearer's left side, *never* on his right side.

Caught in his lie, Bugs gave back the sayings.

Solution to
The Case of the Stolen Tools

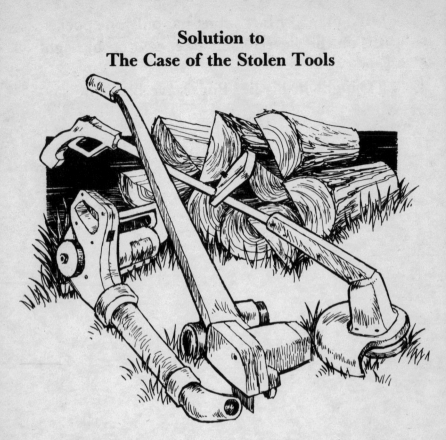

Two hours had passed between the time
Bugs *said* he had looked at the moon through
the telescope and the time Sally did. Impossible!

In two hours the moon would have traveled
past the telescope's field of vision.

Encyclopedia reasoned: After hearing him
and Sally talking about the party as they
walked past his house, Bugs stole the tools, hid

them, and called the police. However, Officer Clancy did not arrive for two hours.

When Bugs saw him coming, he aimed the telescope at the moon. Then, pretending to be Stan Hemming, he telephoned Sally and got the detectives to enter his backyard.

Because he knew nothing about astronomy, Bugs's attempt to frame the detectives went *flop*!

Solution to
The Case of the Angry Girl

Lulubelle, a third-grader, wrote down Tyrone's message "word for word." But he forgot to punctuate it for her!

So, as Encyclopedia realized, Lulubelle put in her own commas and periods—in the wrong places.

The commas and periods were so placed as to change Tyrone's meaning entirely and make Adorabelle punching mad!

What Adorabelle read was:

How I long for a girl who understands what true romance is. All about you are sweet and faithful girls who are unlike you. Kiss the first boy who comes along, Adorabelle. I'd like to praise your beauty forever. I can't. Stop thinking you are the prettiest girl alive. Thine,

Tyrone

Solution to
The Case of the *Albatross*

Jim needed to photograph his trout being "caught" unnoticed. So finding *Albatross* alone at Biscayne Landing, he scared the fish and got *Albatross* to leave.

Actually, he photographed a fish frozen in a curved position. Thus, it appeared as if the fish were alive and fighting.

Letting the fish thaw out, he brought it to be judged. The photograph was meant to prove that he had caught the fish during the tournament.

Encyclopedia spotted the clue. A live fish fighting a line sprays water in all directions. The drops of water fell from the fish in the photograph as if from a rock—"downward."

Solution to
The Case of the Prize Pig

Chuck Dawson wanted to give his father's pig the best chance to win.

He knew that the fastest pig in the heats started from the number one chute in the final. So after the heats, he slyly shoved a chocolate chip cookie into the number one chute through the air slot. Hambone broke late because he was eating the cookie when the race started.

Chuck was *leaving*, not arriving, when he

met the detectives in the parking lot. His long cigar ash was proof. The ash would have blown away during the motorcycle trip to the fairgrounds!

Encyclopedia informed the officials. One of them recalled seeing Chuck in the tent during the heats. The final was rerun, and Hambone won.

Solution to
The Case of the Hard-luck Boy

Before answering the last question, Mary McKean had gone for a drink of water—and passed the room with the prizes.

Her curiosity got the better of her. She sneaked in and opened the three boxes. The wristwatch, the first prize, slipped from her hand and broke on the floor.

So Mary decided to try for the second or third prize. She deliberately didn't answer the last question. That was her mistake!

She knew a word with "three double letters in a row." She called herself a *bookkeeper*!

When Encyclopedia told Mary that he had figured out what she had done, she confessed. She gave Arty her prize, the adding machine.

Solution to
The Case of the Giant Watermelon

Encyclopedia performed a simple test: He turned the book upside down. Holding the covers out like the wings of an airplane, he let the pages fall open freely.

Each time he did so, the pages parted differently—except in one place. They always parted between pages 136 and 137.

That was where the chapter on Clive's favorite, Ted Williams, began. Clive had weakened the binding there by reading the chapter over and over.

Faced with the evidence, Clive denied he was the thief till Omar threatened to have his father call Clive's father.

Clive confessed. He returned Milly-Dilly, which he had stolen for the seeds.

Solution to
The Case of the Fighter Kite

When Sally accused her of flying her kite into the clouds, Tessie made up an alibi on the spot.

She said she had just got out of a bubble bath, where she had been soaking for "longer" than an hour.

But then Tessie filed her fingernails!

She completely forgot that she would never file her nails after washing dishes, showering, or bathing. Nails that have been softened in hot or warm water will split or peel when filed.

Encyclopedia pointed out her error, and Tessie became frightened. She begged him not to get her into trouble.

Encyclopedia agreed—if Tessie promised never to fly her kite into the clouds again.

This time Tessie kept her word.

Solution to
The Case of the Mysterious Handprints

Molly Farrow filled the work gloves with cement (both of which she'd stolen) and sewed on straps cut from her belt. Wearing the gloves as sandals, she walked to the house after the rain had stopped, stole the bookends, and returned to the cottage. She wanted everyone to think that the thief was the crippled Jack Maloney—that he had walked on his hands.

She threw the evidence into the canal, planning to recover the bookends at her convenience.

To lift suspicion from herself, she made up the story of her missing gloves. A lie, Encyclopedia realized. No visitor brings leather gloves to Idaville in the summer.

A diver found the bookends, wrapped together in a blouse she had worn the day before. Her second mistake!

She had not reported the blouse missing.

ABOUT THE AUTHOR

DONALD J. SOBOL is the author of the highly acclaimed Encyclopedia Brown books. His awards for these books include the Pacific Northwest Reader's Choice Award for *Encyclopedia Brown Keeps the Peace* and a special Edgar from the Mystery Writers of America for his contribution to mystery writing in the United States.

Donald Sobol is married and has three children. A native of New York, he now lives in Florida.